Rock-a-bye
Baby

and

Rock-a-bye
Puppy

Notes for adults

TADPOLES NURSERY RHYMES are structured to provide support for newly independent readers. The books may also be used by adults for sharing with young children.

The language of nursery rhymes is often already familiar to an emergent reader, so the opportunity to see these rhymes in print gives a highly supportive early reading experience. The alternative rhymes extend this reading experience further, and encourage children to play with language and try out their own rhymes.

If you are reading this book with a child, here are a few suggestions:

1. Make reading fun! Choose a time to read when you and the child are relaxed and have time to share the story.

2. Recite the nursery rhyme together before you start reading. What might the alternative rhyme be about? Why might the child like it?

3. Encourage the child to reread the rhyme, and to retell it in their own words, using the illustrations to remind them what has happened.

4. Point out together the rhyming words when the whole rhymes are repeated on pages 12 and 22 (developing phonological awareness will help with decoding language) and encourage the child to make up their own alternative rhymes.

5. Give praise! Remember that small mistakes need not always be corrected.

First published in 2008 by
Franklin Watts
338 Euston Road
London NW1 3BH

Franklin Watts Australia
Level 17/207 Kent Street
Sydney NSW 2000

Text (Rock-a-bye Puppy)
© Mick Gowar 2008
Illustration © Christina Bretschneider 2008

The rights of Mick Gowar to be identified as the author of Rock-a-bye Puppy and Christina Bretschneider as the illustrator of this Work have been asserted in accordance with the Copyright, Designs and Patents Act, 1988.

ISBN 978 0 7496 8035 0 (hbk)
ISBN 978 0 7496 8041 1 (pbk)

Series Editor: Jackie Hamley
Series Advisor: Dr Hilary Minns
Series Designer: Peter Scoulding

The author and publisher would like to thank Frances Gowar for permission to reproduce the photograph on p. 14.

Printed in China

Franklin Watts is a division of
Hachette Children's Books
an Hachette Livre UK company.
www.hachettelivre.co.uk

Rock-a-bye Baby

Retold by Mick Gowar

Illustrated by Christina Bretschneider

FRANKLIN WATTS
LONDON•SYDNEY

Christina Bretschneider

"This is me with my son
Anton. We both like singing
along to nursery rhymes,
and we love the rhymes
with actions."

Rock-a-bye baby
on the treetop.

When the wind blows,
the cradle will rock.

When the bough breaks,
the cradle will fall.

Down will come baby, cradle and all.

11

Rock-a-bye Baby

Rock-a-bye baby on the treetop.

When the wind blows,

the cradle will rock.

When the bough breaks,

the cradle will fall.

Down will come baby,

cradle and all.

Can you point to the
rhyming words?

Rock-a-bye Puppy

by Mick Gowar
Illustrated by Christina Bretschneider

13

Mick Gowar

"This is me in my shed. This is where I write my books. When I'm not writing I like visiting schools to read my books and tell stories to the children."

Rock-a-bye puppy
up in the sky.

When the wind blows,
he flies up so high.

17

When the wind drops, the basket comes down.

Back will come puppy,
safe on the ground.